ALIENS GET THE SNIFFLES TOO!

AHHH-CHOO!

Katy S. Duffield   illustrated by K. G. Campbell

CANDLEWICK PRESS

Little Alien was sick.

And sick is extra-terrestrial bad when you have
two throats, five ears, and three noses.

"My throats are scratchy," said Little Alien.

"I've got an idea," said Daddy Alien.
He hopped into his spaceship and zoomed away.

"Well, look at that!" Mama Alien cried when he returned.
"It's a Milky Way milkshake!"

Mars Rover barked.
He licked the drip that ran down Little Alien's chin.

"My ears hurt too," said Little Alien.

So Mama Alien scooped a Little Dipperful of water
and added a pinch of stardust.

"Granny Alien's Famous Shooting-Star Ear Drops,"
said Daddy Alien. "That'll put a twinkle in those ears!"

But Mars Rover whined.

"Now my noses are stuffed up," said Little Alien.
"Call in the lunar decongestants!" Daddy Alien cried.

It was not a pretty sight.

Mars Rover growled.
Those guys gave him the cosmic creeps!

Mars Rover was Little Alien's best friend, and seeing Little Alien so sick was worse than forgetting where he'd buried his bone.

"I'm hot and my head hurts," said Little Alien.
So Mama Alien put him under a cool meteor shower.

Then Daddy Alien fluffed Little Alien's space-cloud pillow and tucked him in under his sparkling blanket of stars.

But just when it looked like Little Alien might doze off at last . . .

"Which nose did that come from?" Mama Alien cried.

EARTH-CHOO!

Mars Rover couldn't stand it any longer.
He had to do something to
make Little Alien feel better.

So he began to put on a show.

Little Alien watched.
The corners of his mouth curved upward.

Hurrah! Little Alien had smiled! Now Mars Rover juggled
Saturn's rings using six of his feet and only two of his tails.

Then he tossed a ring onto each of Little Alien's five ears.
A small giggle escaped Little Alien's lips.

For his final trick, Mars Rover soared high, high into the night sky. He clipped a cord onto his asteroid belt and leaped from the glimmering crescent moon.

In three twinkles of the brightest star, Little Alien had a Jupiter-size smile that stretched from one nose to the other.

But then . . .

WOOF!

"Call in the lunar decongestants!" cried Little Alien.

To my sweet mama,
who always took care of me when I was sick
K. S. D.

To Felix and Charley
K. G. C.

First edition 2017

Library of Congress Catalog Card Number pending
ISBN 978-0-7636-6502-9

17 18 19 20 21 22 CCP 10 9 8 7 6 5 4 3 2 1

Printed in Shenzhen, Guangdong, China

This book was typeset in Myriad Pro.
The illustrations were done in pen, watercolor, and colored pencil.

Candlewick Press
99 Dover Street
Somerville, Massachusetts 02144

visit us at www.candlewick.com